Cla Special Wish

WENDY HOBBS

The Claudia Quash Series
The Spell of Pencliff
Claudia's Special Wish

© Wendy Hobbs
www.wendyhobbs.com
Twitter: @WendyFHobbs
Facebook: Facebook.com/ClaudiaQuash

Illustrated by Martine Cucciniello.
www.martinecucciniello.co.uk

Published in the UK by Wendy Hobbs.
The right of the Author to be identified as author of this Work has been asserted
by him in accordance with sections 77 and 78 of the Copyright, Designs and
Patents Act 1988.

A catalogue record for this book is available from the British Library.

Published October 2016
First Edition October 2016

ISBN: 9781539611509

Category: Juvenile Fiction / Fantasy & Magic

I donate all of the profits from the sale of this book to *Dreams & Wishes*, a wonderful charity that cares for seriously ill children and their families.

– Wendy Hobbs

www.dreamsandwishescharity.org

To
Adam
love
Wendy Hobbs

Acknowledgements

I would like to thank my beautiful daughter, Claudia, who has inspired my writing and who makes every day magical!

Claudia's Special Wish

One snowy night at the start of December, Claudia was woken by the distant tinkling of a bell. She got out of bed, confused, and wondered what could be causing the noise. Hurrying to the bedroom window, she opened the curtains to reveal the biggest star in the sky twinkling like a diamond. It looked amazing, unlike any star she'd ever seen before. She wondered if it might be a lucky star, so she closed her eyes and shouted at the top of her voice, 'I wish I could meet Father Christmas in Lapland!'

Just at that moment, her mother passed by her bedroom door and heard Claudia's wish. Claudia was a good girl, and her mother decided to treat her by booking a trip to Lapland for her birthday, which was just a couple of weeks away.

Even though it was difficult, Mum kept the secret a surprise until the night before Claudia's birthday. She finally told her just before Claudia went to bed. Claudia was so happy she could hardly sleep, which made getting up very early in the morning to go to the airport a struggle.

Claudia's alarm clock woke her with a startling jolt at 5:00am. She felt tired, but she quickly realised that they were off on an adventure! It was hard to imagine a greater gift than meeting Father Christmas in his home.

'The taxi is here!' called her mother, heading for the front door.

When they arrived at the airport, Claudia was bursting with excitement. Her head was full of images of crunching snow, cute elves, and Father Christmas holding a sack overflowing with amazing presents.

As soon as the taxi stopped at the airport, Claudia flung open the door. She jumped out and ran into the road, not looking where she was going.

Without warning, a car passed the parked taxi and accidentally hit her! The car screeched to a halt.

'Claudia!' cried her mother as she rushed around the car. 'Claudia, are you alright?'

Claudia didn't hear her mother. Her world had already gone dark.

* * *

Later that day, Claudia woke up, feeling fuzzy-headed. She looked around and realised with disappointment that she wasn't in Lapland, but in bed, in a white-walled hospital room glittering with Christmas decorations. She was in a pink nightdress, and she had a bandage wrapped around her sore head.

'W-what happened?' she asked as a blurry figure came into view.

'I'm sorry, darling,' said her mother, who was standing next to the bed. 'You got hit by a car.'

'Oh no!' sobbed Claudia, rubbing her head through the bandages. 'Does that mean we won't be going to Lapland?'

'I'm afraid we missed the flight,' replied her mother.

Claudia's eyes filled with tears. She couldn't believe how stupid she had been.

'If only I'd been more careful getting out of the taxi!' she moaned.

Her mum brushed Claudia's fringe with her fingers.

'Don't get upset. There's always next year.'

After that, she stayed a while and they talked about Christmas, but soon she had to go. Standing up, she buttoned up her coat and said, 'Try and get some rest. I'll see you in the morning.'

Claudia settled back in her bed and sighed. Her head ached and she felt sick. She rolled onto her side and gazed through a chink in the curtains of her hospital room at the starry sky, until her eyes finally closed and she fell fast asleep.

* * *

During the night, a jingling noise rang out in the darkness.

Claudia's eyes popped open. As she looked around the dark room, she frowned. A strange sound was coming from outside. Through the slightly open curtains she could see the bright star from a couple of weeks before. Amazingly, it was flashing! It shot a beam of rainbow-coloured light through the window, which landed on the bathroom door next to her bed, making it glow.

Claudia was mesmerised. She slowly climbed out of bed, and for some reason, she suddenly felt completely better – no headache, no nausea. She didn't know why, but something inside her – a strange force – was telling her that this was no ordinary light. Moving cautiously towards it, she pushed open the door then gasped.

She wasn't inside the bathroom, but instead she was sinking into deep, crisp, white snow in a beautiful pine forest. And her clothes had changed. She was now dressed in a warm, purple coat and wore polished black boots.

Claudia's eyes widened in surprise.

In the distance she could see a reindeer galloping towards her, pulling what looked like a sleigh. As they approached, she spotted that the driver was a tiny man in a green suit and a pointed red hat. His rosy cheeks sported a big smile.

When the sleigh stopped beside her, the reindeer shook his head, snorted, and pawed at the ground.

'Would you like to meet Father Christmas?' called out the happy little man.

'F-Father Christmas,' repeated Claudia disbelievingly. 'He's here?'

'Of course! You asked to see him, didn't you?'

Claudia gulped and took a step back. She remembered wishing on a big star before her accident.

'I did, but I never imagined that he'd hear me. Does that mean you're...?'

'An elf? Yes,' he smiled. 'The name's Figgy. I've worked for Father Christmas for many years making toys and trinkets for the children.'

'OK,' said Claudia. She took a deep breath and carefully climbed into the gleaming sleigh. It was piled high with wrapped presents.

'We're off!' shouted the elf, pulling on the reins.

As they lurched forward, he recited a magical spell in a strange language. Snow circled the sleigh and it lifted them off the ground in a swirl of silver sparks. Soaring through the blue sky, Claudia held on tightly. Below them she saw the beautiful Northern Lights dancing around the stars.

'Watch out! Hold on!' warned the elf, as they just missed the moon.

Claudia gripped the plush seat under her to stay steady. She never imagined that she would be having such a wild time, flying through the sky with the stars lighting their path.

They flew for miles and the sleigh eventually descended towards a pretty village blanketed in snow. It was set amongst a frozen forest and the trees were draped in twinkling blue lights and shimmering snowflakes. They glided over the village, and above the tree tops, following a footpath far below. It led them to a snow-covered cabin in a small clearing. A trail of smoke rose gently from the chimney and a pair of ice skates lay by the front door.

'This is a very secret place,' whispered Figgy as they landed with a bump, 'Only special children are invited here.'

'Really?' said Claudia, surprised that anyone would think that she was special. She leapt off the sleigh, rushed towards the door, and pushed it open.

'Welcome, Claudia!' boomed a cheerful voice.

Claudia's face lit up the moment she noticed the rounded man with the crimson coat and a white beard. Father Christmas was sitting in a rocking chair next to a roaring fire, warming his hands. In a corner of the room was a Christmas tree decorated with tinsel and bright golden bows.

'I'm so glad you could make it,' he said, standing to greet her.

Claudia's mouth fell open. 'Are you really Father Christmas?'

'Yes, I am,' he said, chuckling. 'I heard that you had to go to the hospital.'

'How did you know about my accident?'

'Father Christmas knows everything,' he said, smiling back at her. 'How are you feeling now?'

'I feel wonderful!' said Claudia, brimming with joy.

'Come and warm yourself by the fire,' he urged. 'I have something for you.'

Claudia quickly sat beside Father Christmas and he handed her a small wooden box tied with a red ribbon.

'Thank you,' said Claudia, eager to see what it was.

She opened the present and lifted out a sparkling silver bell. It was engraved with wings and hung from a fine, silver chain.

'It's an angel bell,' said Father Christmas. 'The elves make them each year for the children.'

Claudia's eyes glistened. It was the most beautiful necklace she had ever seen.

'Every time an angel bell rings, a child's wish is granted,' said Father Christmas.

Claudia couldn't believe her ears. She remembered hearing a bell on the night that she had made a wish on the biggest star in the sky.

'Have something to eat,' said Father Christmas, handing her a plate with sugar-coated cookies.

Claudia tucked into the delicious biscuits. Their buttery goodness soon filled her stomach and she yawned.

'You've travelled a long way,' said Father Christmas, handing her a soft, green blanket. 'Have a little sleep now. I'll wake you up when Figgy arrives with the sleigh to take you home.'

As if by magic, Claudia felt her eyes burning and she sank into her cosy chair. She wrapped the blanket around her and quickly fell fast asleep.

* * *

A few hours later, Claudia woke to someone stroking her hand and gently calling her name.

'Claudia… Claudia… It's time to go home.'

'Is the sleigh here?' she mumbled, opening her eyes.

'What did you say?' asked her mother.

14

Claudia sat up in bed and looked around the room. 'Where's Father Christmas?' she asked.

'Father Christmas? You must have been dreaming, darling.'

Claudia wrinkled her nose. 'But it seemed so real. There was a friendly elf called Figgy... and we flew through the air on a sleigh full of presents. It was so exciting!'

'Never mind, sweetheart,' replied her mother. 'At least you had a nice rest.'

'Yeah, I suppose you're right...' she agreed.

'You're looking so much better now, and the doctor says that you can come home today.'

Next moment, the door opened and a nurse walked in. She spoke quietly to Claudia's mum. 'Can I have a quick word with you before you leave?'

'I won't be a moment,' said Claudia's mother, disappearing out of the door. 'You get dressed, Claudia.'

As Claudia got out of bed, she felt sad that she hadn't been on a magical adventure. Dragging the duvet into place, she ran her hand over something metallic. When she pulled the curious object from under the covers, she broke into a beaming smile. It was the sparkling angel bell.

So it wasn't a dream! she thought.

She held the necklace to her ear and rang the bell, thinking of the twinkling star and the special wish she had made.

'It was all true,' she squealed happily. 'I did go to Lapland. And I did meet Father Christmas!'

Goodbye from Figgy!

THE END

Help an Author!

Dear Reader,

Now that you've read *Claudia's Special Wish* I would really appreciate it if you reviewed it on Amazon. Great reviews sell books and the more books sold the more the charity will benefit from the funds raised! Support me by writing a review today. It would be extremely helpful!

Wendy Hobbs